The toys were sick with worry today. Not only were they moving to a new house soon, but this very afternoon Andy was having a birthday party. And parties with gifts spelled bad news for the toys. They could be replaced!

Woody turned to the toy soldiers.

"SERGEANT — establish a RECON POST downstairs.

CODE RED. You know what to do."

An army of green soldiers parachuted into the hallway, and reported back by baby speaker. Andy got a lunchbox, bed sheets, a boardgame. Nothing to worry about, until…

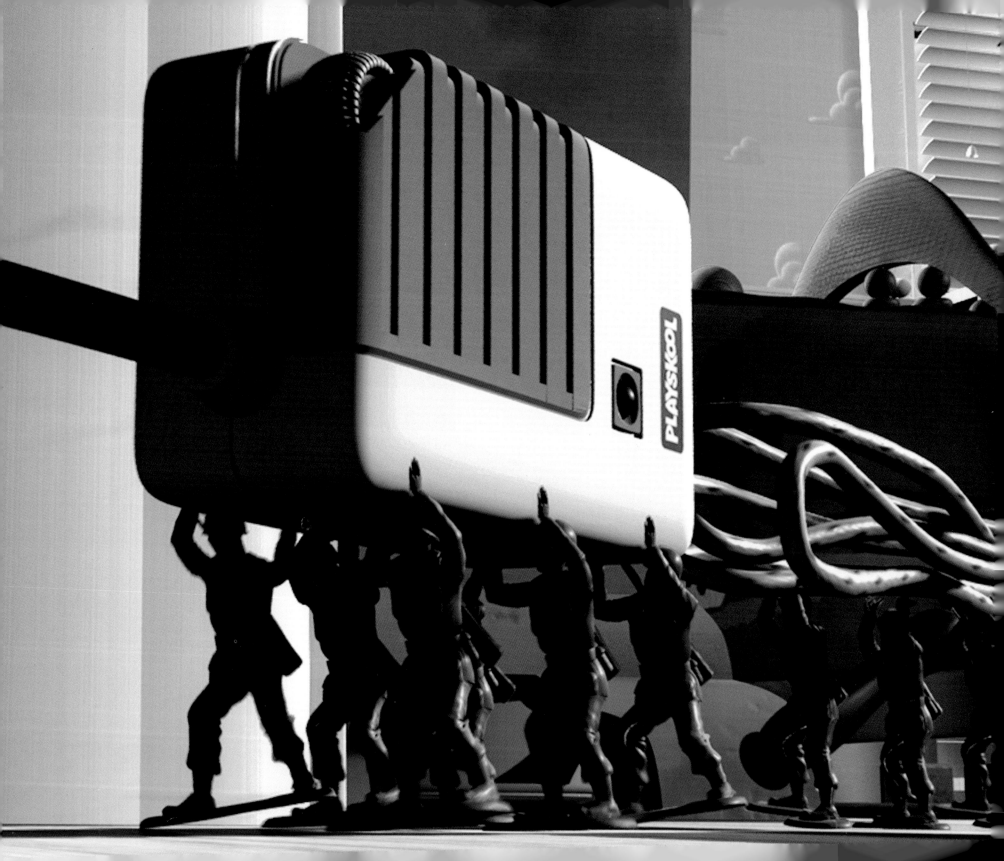

Come in, Mother Bird, come in. Mom has pulled a surprise present from the closet. Andy's opening it…"
The next thing Woody knew, Andy and his friends had pounded up the stairs, flung him to the floor, and replaced him with

Buzz Lightyear,
Space Ranger.

"To infinity and beyond!" crowed Andy, repeating Buzz's famous motto.
Woody felt awful.
He told Buzz, "There has been a bit of a mix-up. This is my spot, see, the bed here…"

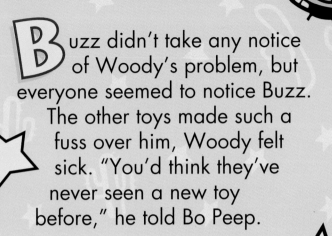

Buzz didn't take any notice of Woody's problem, but everyone seemed to notice Buzz. The other toys made such a fuss over him, Woody felt sick. "You'd think they've never seen a new toy before," he told Bo Peep.

But this was
NO ORDINARY TOY!

As Bo Peep told Woody, "He's got more gadgets on him than a swiss army knife."
That did it. "Listen, Lightsnack," Woody said in disgust, "you stay away from Andy! He's mine, and no one is taking him away from me!"

Determined to be Andy's number-one toy, Woody knew he was facing a major threat. Andy and his mom were going to Pizza Planet for dinner. Only one toy could go along. "Will Andy pick me?" Woody asked the Magic 8 Ball. "Don't count on it," came the answer.

For Woody there was only one solution— **do away with** ~~BUZZ LIGHTYEAR.~~

Woody could hit him with a remote-control car! Yeah! But Buzz saw the car coming and jumped out of the way—only to fall out of the window!

Whirrr!!!" went the remote-control car. "RC is telling us this was no accident," Mr. Potato Head said. "Buzz was pushed...by Woody." The toys were furious.

"Let's STRING  HIM UP by his pull-string!"

said Mr. Potato Head. It seemed like curtains for Woody when Andy ran in. But Andy couldn't find Buzz. "Honey, just grab some other toy!" shouted Andy's mom from downstairs. Andy grabbed Woody. Woody was again Andy's main man and safe from the others—or so he thought.

Just as the car pulled out of the driveway, Buzz Lightyear leaped on the back. The car stopped at a gas station and Buzz hopped in. He glared at Woody. "I just want you to know that even though you tried to terminate me, revenge is not an idea we promote on my planet."

"Oh. Oh, that's good," Woody said with relief.

"But we're not on my planet, are we?"

asked Buzz. Then Buzz tore into Woody, and Woody fought back, until the two of them fell out on the street. That was when the car drove away.

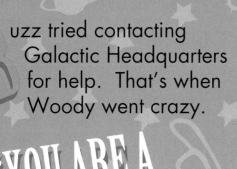

uzz tried contacting Galactic Headquarters for help. That's when Woody went crazy.

"YOU ARE A

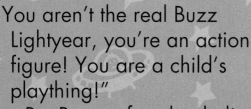

TOY!

You aren't the real Buzz Lightyear, you're an action figure! You are a child's plaything!"

But Buzz refused to believe him. Even after the two managed to get themselves to Pizza Planet, Buzz was still looking for a spaceship to take him home. And he found one—a rocket-shaped crane game filled with alien toys. Buzz jumped in. Woody went after him. And Andy's cruel neighbor Sid took the controls.

A Buzz Lightyear! No way!"
yelled Sid. The claw grabbed
Buzz, while Woody tried to pull
Buzz away. But it was hopeless.
Sid got them both. "All right!
Double prizes!"

Woody tried to warn Buzz
about Sid. "Once we go into Sid's
house, we won't be coming out."
Buzz wouldn't listen until he
witnessed one of Sid's home
operations—taking toys apart and
putting them back together all
mixed up. Then Buzz started
yelling for help,

"Come in, Star Command!
Send
reinforcements!"

No one came, but Buzz and
Woody did find a way out of
Sid's bedroom.

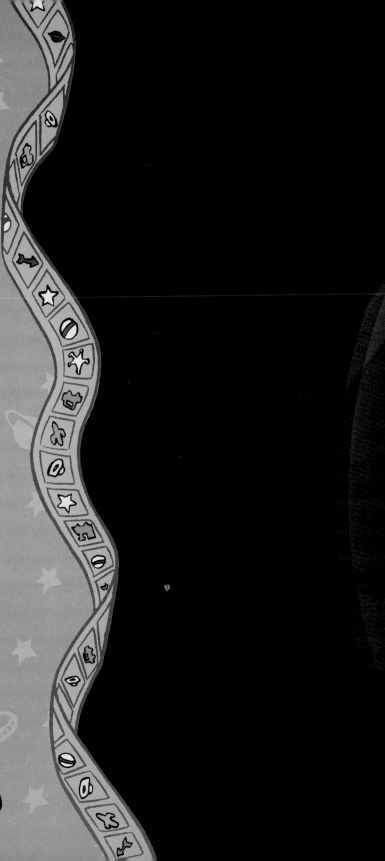

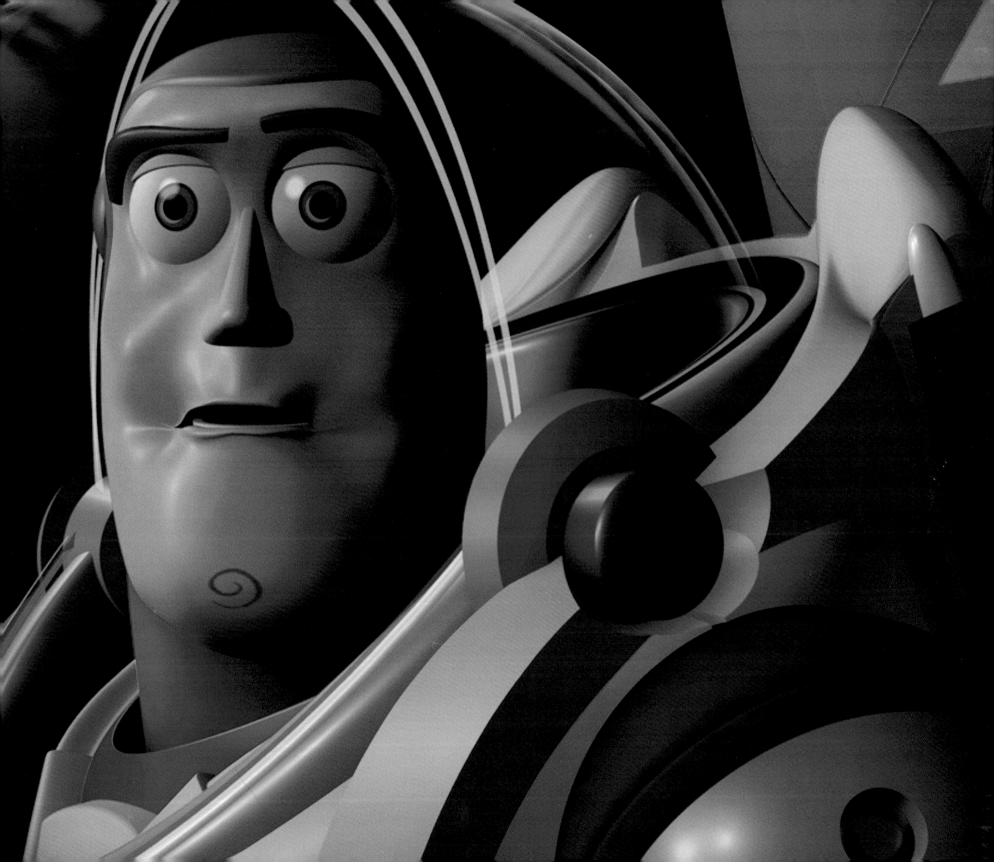

Out in the hallway, Buzz yelled, "Split up!" and headed for the den. That's when he heard,

"Calling

Buzz Lightyear.

This is

Star Command."

Buzz was thrilled until he realized the voice was coming from the TV. "Yes, kids—Buzz Lightyear. The world's greatest superhero is now the world's greatest toy!" Suddenly Buzz remembered Woody's words, "You are a toy!" Woody had been right, and it was more than Buzz could take. When Sid tied Buzz to a rocket, ready to shoot him to infinity and beyond, Buzz didn't even care.

But Woody wouldn't give up! He looked at Buzz and said, "Look! Over in that house is a kid who thinks you are the greatest...you are his toy!"

Thinking of Andy, Buzz pulled himself together—but not in time to save himself. Sid had Buzz outside, tied to the rocket, when a most extraordinary thing happened. Led by Woody, an army of mutant toys confronted Sid, sending him into the house screaming!

Woody ran to help Buzz, freeing him just as the moving truck and family van took off from Andy's house. Woody and Buzz gave chase in a toy car. They were about to catch up with Andy and his family when the car's batteries ran out, leaving them stranded.

Thinking fast, Woody lit the rocket on Buzz's back, sending them blasting into the sky. They rocketed through the sunroof of the van, landing right beside Andy, who let out a happy yell.

"Woody! Buzz!"

And so it was that Andy was reunited with both his favorite toys who were now friends

"to infinity and beyond!"